Rachel Sibey
Jennifer Glossop
Angela Douglas
Freda Nicholls
Alan Jenkins
Mark Billen

*To thank you all*
*for teaching my children*

SIMON AND SCHUSTER BOOKS FOR YOUNG READERS
Simon & Schuster Building, Rockefeller Center
1230 Avenue of the Americas, New York, New York 10020

Library of Congress Cataloging-in-Publication Data
Buchanan, Heather S.   George and Matilda Mouse and the
floating school.   Summary: After a scary encounter with the
cat, a class of mice finds a safer location for its school
[1.  Schools—Fiction.  2.  Mice—Fiction]  I.  Title.
PZ7.B87713Ge  1990     [E]     89-22036
ISBN 0-671-70613-6

# George and Matilda Mouse
## and the Floating School

### Heather S. Buchanan

Simon and Schuster Books for Young Readers

Published by Simon & Schuster Inc., New York

There was once a dolls' house tucked away in a quiet corner of an old garden. It had real glass windows and a tin door.

Inside lived George and Matilda Mouse and their five children, Parsley, Mallow, Periwinkle, Columbine and Polyanthus. The Mouse family slept all day and worked and played all night.

The little mice were sometimes very noisy, but inside the dolls' house they were safe from the cat.

Matilda Mouse wanted her children to play with other little mice. And she wanted them to learn how to read. But there was no school.

Matilda decided she would start her own school. But a school needed pupils. Fergus, a very old mouse who lived nearby in a gardener's boot, had once told George and Matilda about the rock garden mice. They lived by a pond in the middle of the garden.

That night George and Matilda left the children with Fergus and set out to visit the rock garden mice.

Behind a door in the rock garden, a ladder of twigs led down into a snug burrow. After introducing herself and George, Matilda invited the little rock garden mice to come and learn their lessons with her children in the dolls' house school.

The clever rock garden mice already knew the names of all the plants in the garden. But they quickly agreed to send their little mice to school. Grandmother Lobelia would bring the first pupils the very next night.

The moon was shining brightly as Lobelia and the little mice set out across the slippery rocks on their way to school. Suddenly there was a big splash. Dandelion tried to leap over two rocks and fell, paws over tail, into the pond.

Lobelia lowered Lavender on her walking stick and she grabbed Dandelion just before the goldfish got him. Back on the rock Lobelia hugged Dandelion dry and wrapped him warmly in her shawl.

It was a tired little group that finally knocked on the dolls' house door.

Matilda began lessons in the nursery. She used the dolls'
abacus to teach arithmetic. But the rock garden mice were
much more interested in the dolls' house toys.

Matilda decided to teach cooking instead. She took the
little mice down to the kitchen where George was in charge
of lessons. But he couldn't find enough pots and pans for
each mouse to use so he started an art lesson.

The little mice did paw painting using berry jam. When
Matilda returned she found George looking very annoyed
and all the mice covered in jam.

George also taught the little mice to read, using scraps of newspaper that he collected from the garbage can. Soon they knew all the words on the labels of tin cans and candy wrappers.

George thought the mice should learn more about the plants, flowers and insects outside. Helped by the older mice, he built a twig shelter next to the dolls' house where the little mice could have nature study lessons.

The mice did arithmetic by counting the spots on ladybugs—until the bugs wandered off to find new leaves to eat.

Sometimes friendly worms curved themselves into letter shapes so the mice could spell  new words.

And once a spider showed them how to weave a web, but when the little mice tried to copy it with thread they got all tangled up.

One day during a nature lesson Bramble sang a song he made up about a bee. It was such a nice song that Matilda didn't want to stop him. But as his little voice rose higher and higher, what she had always dreaded happened. The cat found them!

The mice scurried away in all directions but poor Bramble was caught! Matilda and Fergus hid nearby, waiting for their chance to help him.

George grabbed a stick.
"Oh, please be careful,"
Matilda squeaked.

George strode out in front of the cat, waving his
stick and squeaking loudly. Immediately the cat's eyes
turned on him. With a growl she sprang forward,
letting go of Bramble.

As George danced around in front of the cat,
Matilda rushed forward and dragged Bramble away.

Just then George tripped and dropped his stick. The cat's
claw snagged his overalls and flicked him in the air. George
caught a glimpse of snapping yellow teeth as he fell into
a bush.

The cat was still crouched, waiting for him. When George
looked around, he saw a familiar sight—the garbage can!
He made a dash for it, but the cat got there first!

She chased poor George around and around the garbage
can. Then she jumped up on top of it to dive down on him.
But the lid was loose, and as the cat sprang up, it tipped
over and the whole can crashed down.

The cat yowled and ran away.

George lay frightened but safe under the garbage can lid.
Slowly a big smile spread across his face, for out of the can
had tumbled something truly wonderful!

George made his way cautiously back along the flower bed
to the dolls' house. Before he got there, he heard squeaks of
joy and relief and through the ivy rushed his family.

Matilda hugged George and took him to see little Bramble,
who was sipping tea in the nursery while Lobelia scurried
around bandaging his scratches.

Later that night there was a knock at the door. Outside was a small group of rock garden mice. News of the disaster had reached them and the little mice had been forbidden to return to school.

Matilda wept. The school would have to close.

George smiled mysteriously, handed some strong rope to the rock garden mice, and told them all to follow him.

When they got to the garbage can, George pushed aside some apple peels and stood back proudly to show Matilda what he had found—a toy Noah's Ark.

"It's a new school," he announced happily. "A floating school!"

At dawn the mice worked hard to drag the Ark
to the pond and anchor it securely. They made
paddles and seats for the inside.

They painted pictures for the walls and stored food in the cupboards. There was a peg for each little mouse to hang up his life jacket and a locker for pens and paper.

When the floating school was ready, the proud mice rowed it across the pond to collect the pupils for the first lessons aboard the Ark.

For George and Matilda it was a dream come true.
Now the mice could add pond life to their list of
things to study. Fergus promised swimming lessons.
   But best of all, the cat never interrupted them again,
because, of course, cats hate getting their paws wet!